Chicken Bedtime Is Really Early

written by **Erica S. Perl**   illustrated by **George Bates**

HARRY N. ABRAMS, INC., PUBLISHERS

ACKNOWLEDGMENTS

Thank you to my family and friends for their love and encouragement. Thanks also to Susan Van Metre, Susan Kaufman, and Adrienne Brodeur. And thanks to Mr. Rivers, Jr., as promised.

In addition, special thanks to Kenna Kay. It is not often that someone comes along who is a true friend and an astute observer of chickens. Kenna is both.
—E.S.P.

The images in this book were created using acrylic paint and a masking technique.

Designer: Becky Terhune
Production Manager: Jonathan Lopes

Library of Congress Cataloging-in-Publication Data:
Perl, Erica S.
Chicken bedtime / Erica S. Perl ; illustrated by George Bates.
p. cm.
Summary: Rhyming text describes how different animal mothers and fathers get their young ones ready for bed on the farm.
ISBN 0-8109-4926-1 (alk. paper)
[1. Bedtime—Fiction. 2. Domestic animals—Fiction. 3. Domestic animals—Infancy—Fiction. 4. Parent and child—Fiction. 5. Stories in rhyme.] I. Bates, George, ill. II. Title.
PZ8.3.P4225Chi 2004
[E]—dc22
2004001464

Printed and bound in China
2 4 6 8 10 9 7 5 3 1

Harry N. Abrams, Inc.
100 Fifth Avenue
New York, NY 10011
www.abramsbooks.com

Abrams is a subsidiary of
LA MARTINIÈRE
GROUPE

For Mike, Franny, and Bougie

—E.S.P.

To my sister Mary

—G.B.

From chickens to hamsters, from rabbits to sheep,
Sooner or later we all need to sleep.
At five o'clock, chickens get ready for bed,
Each spotted white hen and each Rhode Island Red.

The chicks take their baths, chicken moms standing near,
To make sure they wash behind each chicken ear.

Now fluffy and dry, the chicks bounce into bed.
The moms cluck good night and give pecks on the head.

So when it is six, every chick boy and girlie,
Is snug in the coop. Chicken bedtime is early!

At seven, it's time for the cows and the sheep,
To call their young into the barn for some sleep.

The lambs and the calves are all running and playing,
Not listening to what their mamas are saying.

One minute, the barn door is swung open wide.
Next minute, it's closed—with the mamas inside!

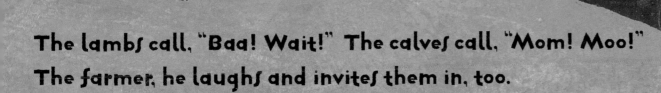

The lambs call, "Baa! Wait!" The calves call, "Mom! Moo!"
The farmer, he laughs and invites them in, too.

At eight, it is time for the bunnies to stop,
Their chewing and chomping and hop hop hop hop!

It's time for each one of the
bun-dads and mommies,
To put their young rabbits
in footy pajamies.

Then into the rabbit hole, into the pile.
"Who kicked me?" says one with a mischievous smile.

"A story! A story!" the young bunnies roar.
And just as it ends, all the bunnies beg, "More!"
(Although they've all heard it eighteen times before.)

At nine o'clock, fishes are ending their day,
Each eel, every minnow, each snapper and ray.

Those that have teeth, well,
they give them a brush.
Those that do not, well,
they gargle and such.

Then some of the little fish sons and fish daughters,
Ask, "Why can't I have just one more glass of water?"

The fish dads are stern. "No more carping, I said!
You've got school in the morning. Come on. Off to bed!"

At ten, it is time for the frogs to take five,
And rest from the concert that they perform live.

The croaking and singing of songs so inspired,
Results in a pond full of frogs who are tired.

So frog moms and pops get the tadpoles all fed,
And settle them into their lily pad beds.

Then, in the soft shimmering light of the moon,
An old bullfrog belts out one last froggy tune.

Eleven's the time when the hamsters take rest . . .

At twelve, they're back up, at their hamstery best!
Refreshed from their nap, all the hamsters now feel,
Like taking a brisk midnight jog on the wheel.

Now, one o'clock isn't a bedtime, you see.
Nor, for that matter, is two, or is three.

At those times, most creatures are fast, fast asleep,
Except for the hamsters—what hours they keep!

At four in the morning, the rooster, he rises,
Does push-ups and curl-ups with weights
of all sizes.

He climbs up the fence post and crows at the sun,
Announcing to all that the day has begun.

The chicks all get up at the break of the dawn.
They wake up their mothers, who grumble and yawn.
The cows will soon get up and call, "Morning, moo!"
The bunnies will wake up and hop to it, too.

Later, sheep...frogs...fishes...

AND YOU.
(Wait, who's asleep now?
    You'll never guess who!)